Quentin Blake

The Weed

The world was becoming hard and dry, and more and more difficult to live in; and then one day, without any warning, a deep crack opened in the earth and the Meadowsweet family were at the bottom of it.

All the family were there: Mr and
Mrs Meadowsweet, Marco and Lily,
and Octavia the mynah bird in her cage.

"What do we do now?" said Mrs
Meadowsweet.

"You could start by letting me out of here,"
said Octavia.

All mynah birds can talk, but Octavia talked
more than most.

"At least Octavia can be free," said Lily.

"Perhaps she might get some help," said Marco. "If there's anyone up there."

Octavia flew up towards the patch of sky far above them.

They did not have to wait long, and when Octavia
came back what did she have in her beak?

It was a seed.

Octavia dropped the
seed into a tiny crack in
the rock floor.

Two minutes later a small green plant appeared.

"This isn't going to help us much,"
said Mrs Meadowsweet. "It's only
a weed."

"Never mind that," said Octavia.
"Just stand clear."

The little plant started to grow.

In no time it
became taller,

and taller,

and taller,

and started to put out all
kinds of strange leaves.

It was bigger than any weed they had ever seen.

Octavia said, "Maybe you should start climbing."

They clambered up holding on
to whatever the weed sprouted.
Sometimes it was almost as though it was
putting out green hands to help them.

They climbed and climbed.

Mr Meadowsweet said, "I hope there's something left to eat when we get up there. I'm starving."

Then they noticed that the weed was growing strange green fruit.

Octavia gave a peck or two and said,
"I think you should try them."

"Tastes like peaches," said Mr Meadowsweet.

"Pomegranates," said Mrs Meadowsweet.

"Pineapple," said Lily.

Marco said, "Chocolate banana fudge."

And then Mrs Meadowsweet,
reaching out for another delicious
green fruit, lost her grip and fell.

She landed on a large and comfortable leaf. Long
tendrils wound themselves around her and gently
drew her up to join the rest of the family.

They started to climb again, but by now
the weed was growing faster and faster.

Octavia said, "I think you should
probably just hold on tight."

The weed shot up, getting bigger and bigger
and taller and taller until –

– it burst out above the ground and the Meadowsweet family found themselves thrown onto their hands and knees with greenery sprouting all around them.

They sat and stared around
with amazement.

"Octavia," said Lily. "Did you know
all this was going to happen?"

But, for once, Octavia
said nothing.

For Greenpeace and its supporters.

First published 2020 by order of the Tate Trustees
by Tate Publishing, a division of Tate Enterprises Ltd,
Millbank, London SW1P 4RG
www.tate.org.uk/publishing

This paperback edition published 2021

A catalogue record for this book is available from the British Library

ISBN 978 1 84976 745 3

Distributed in the United States and Canada by ABRAMS, New York
Library of Congress Control Number applied for

Colour reproduction by DL Imaging Ltd, London
Printed and bound in China by C&C Offset Printing Co., Ltd